BLACK TIGHTS

BLACK TIGHTS

POETRY X

Poetry X = Adult Passion Poetry

Poems by: C.S. Blue

Published by

ARROWCLOUD
PRESS

BLACK TIGHTS

Copyright © 2013 by C.S. Blue

(C.S. Blue / C. Steven Blue
is the pen name for Steven C. Schreiner)

ISBN 0-9635499-4-4 / ISBN 978-0-9635499-4-5

First Edition

Editor: Michele Graf
Proofreaders:
Paulette Schreiner
Jennifer Chambers

Drawing: *Bronze Affair* © 1989
by C. Steven Blue

Published by

For orders and information go to
www.wordsongs.com

BLACK
TIGHTS

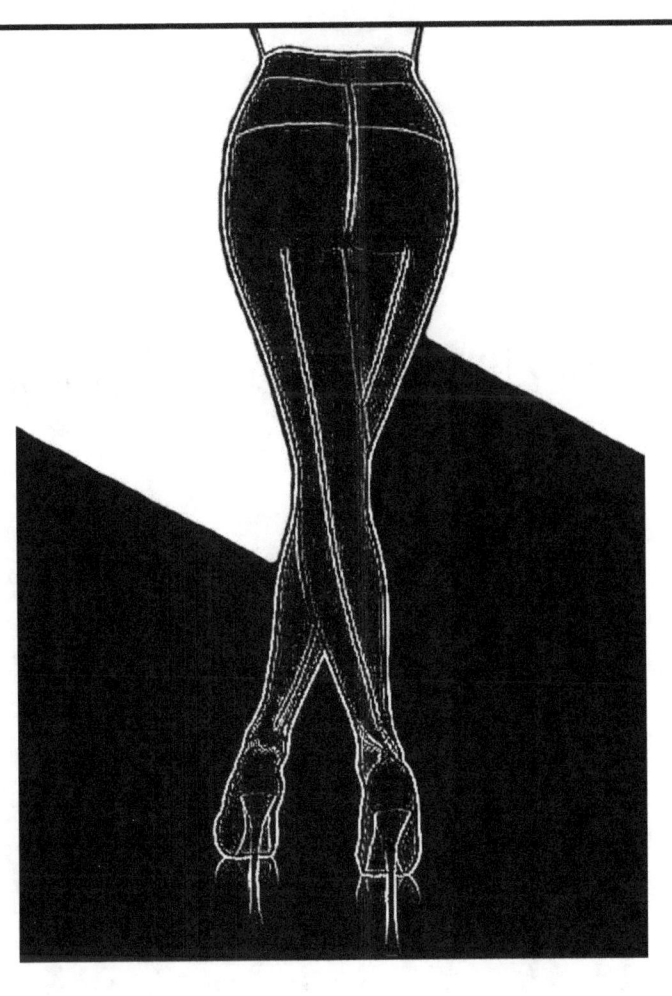

Black Tights:

A passionate journey —

A linear story told in poetry —

Tales of love, lust and romance —

BLACK TIGHTS— *PROLOGUE*

In Southern California . . .
the boys look forward
to summer time

> because . . .
> there is nothing like the girls . . . in bikinis
> on Southern California beaches

But in Oregon . . .
the boys look forward
to winter time

> because . . .
> there is nothing like the girls . . . in black tights
> holiday shopping

BLACK TIGHTS

It's winter time
in Eugene
girls in black tights
drive you crazy

The cutest ass
you've ever seen
seems to walk by
daily

On her way to college
or browsing at the mall
womanhood in all her prime
bound to make you fall

Fall for glory
fall for grace
fall for the beauty
of the human race

You know it's just
a fantasy
but oh, what a dream
it could be

It's Christmas time
in the Great Northwest
the girls in black tights
are out

Struttin' their stuff
all around town
warm and cozy
roundabout

College girls
with fresh winter flush
spark thoughts
that make you blush

In their skin tight vestige
they call . . .
bound to make you
      fall

Fall for glory
fall for grace
fall for the beauty
of the human race

You know it's just
a fantasy
but oh, what a dream
it could be

It's winter time
in Eugene
girls in black tights
drive you crazy

The cutest ass
you've ever seen
seems to walk by
daily

BLACK TIGHTS— *AFTERGLOW*

You . . .
walked on by
with a sideways glance

I . . .
knew that you
knew I was watching you

I wished . . .
oh how I wished
I knew what you were thinking

From out of the blue . . . you appeared
I saw you . . .
From across the room
My eyes were fixed like magnets
A breeze drew me to your perfume

You strolled towards me . . .
With purpose
Your smile lit up the whole place
You seemed to see me . . . the way I saw you
It was written all over your face

So . . .
Come to me my blooming rose
Carry me away
        I propose
Sing me your beauty
In soft spoken words
Teach me the way of love's prose

Out of thin air . . . we created
Love that was destined to be
It happened so quick
—In a time freeze—
Waves of love crashed on the sea

I brought you out of slow yearning
To heightened flames of desire
You lit me so hot . . .
I burned on the spot
And nothing could put out the fire

So . . .
Come to me my blooming rose
Carry me away
        I propose
Sing me your beauty
In soft spoken words
Teach me the way of love's prose

CADILLAC—

I see you move to the rhythm
Flip your long hair to one side
You glance toward me as I find you
Seductive movements in your stride

Coming closer . . .
My heart beats fast
I can't wait for you to speak
I worry each moment
Will be the last
You gently kiss me on my cheek
    . . . And I feel weak

Cadillac—
I want to cruise with you
Soft and supple
Tender and true
Give me more
Open up your door
And take me in . . .
    Again

We share some passion
In the dark
Your eyes stare . . . right into me
Your flowing movements
Make me melt
You're soft as woman can be

I want to take you
All the way
And know you true
In this moment
Surprise me . . . tantalize me
You warm to my touch
As your nipples toughen up

Cadillac—
I want to cruise with you
Soft and supple
Tender and true
Give me more
Open up your door
And take me in . . .
    Again

Goose bumps . . . I feel
On your sylphlike skin
Caressing your neck
As you kiss hot with sin
Come closer . . . come closer
Keep it right here
Don't want it to end
'Cause I'm new again

Cadillac—
I want to cruise with you
Soft and supple
Tender and true
Give me more
Open up your door
And take me in . . .
    Again

If I could speak
from the power of observation
it would be closing in
on your sweet pink passion
        as it . . .
gleams from the sheen
of anticipation.

It's the journey
of the lotus blossom . . . blooming
as you enter the realm
of intimate passage.

Box O' Rox
reveals its mystery
driven by purity
white as snow.

Box O' Rox
is a mystical giant
the only limit
is your mind.

Turquoise, amber
amethyst, jade
oblong longing
in sapphire blue.

Capture before closing
acknowledge the shudder

surrender to the heat
of what becomes you.

If you yearned for greater measure
I would stretch . . . to feel your love
push aside the pink lace wrapture
of your moist pink sigh
            as it . . .
heightens my great longing
for your love.

It's the journey
of the lotus flower . . . falling
the more you pull it apart
the more it becomes.

Box O' Rox
reveals its mystery
driven by pleasure
hot as the sun.

Box O' Rox
is a mystical giant
the only limit
is the sky.

Turquoise, amber
amethyst, jade
oblong longing
in sapphire blue.

Capture before closing
acknowledge the shudder
surrender to the heat
of what becomes you.

I lay here in our love bed
think for awhile
reflect on that special touch
remember your smile
there's a feeling
deep inside you
when everything's okay
I feel that way with you
          now
I hope it stays that way

Seen so seldom
time's been told
visions of . . .
and dreams of old
bring it now
this time speak true
side by side . . . love
me and you

Is this the awakening reign
of love's ever flowing stream
          the one I envision
. . . or do I dream

Are you just another . . .
Pretty picture on my wall
Another memory of love's call
Another photograph
Of another fall
In my gallery of girls
        In my hall

You called me . . .
From out of the blue
You asked If I ever
Still think of you
You asked if you ever hurt me
. . . If only you knew

But it doesn't matter
It would be worth all the hurt
If I could see you . . . be with you
Just one more time . . . when it was our time

BLACK TIGHTS —

EROTIC THOUGHTS —

DREAMS OF PASSION —

FORGET ME NOTS —

SPARKLING WONDER

I gaze at you
Through the crowd
I wonder what it is
. . . Draws me to you

I can see in your eyes
That you feel it too
Every time you have a chance
. . . You glance at me

You are striking
In my eyes
But you could be my demise
Shall I play the fool again

Dark-haired beauty
With long flowing curls
Speak to me
With grace and glory

I yearn to know the story
In your eyes
If you would warm me
With your surprise

I can see you . . .
Shimmer there
Are you aware
How I feel

Do you really
Feel it too
    Could you
    Would you

Tell me sparkling wonder
What is it makes you shine
Why am I drawn to you
Wanting you . . . to want me

Dark-haired beauty
With long flowing curls
Speak to me
With grace and glory

I yearn to know the story
In your eyes
If you would warm me
With your surprise

I've anticipated you
All night long
Your blue dress
    Lover
Hangs on the song
Of my moaning

I stroke you wistfully
Down you I glide

Your hungry eyes pierce me
. . . Deep inside

The cool night has brought us
To this pose
Lingering by the mirror
        It shows

The passion of our kiss
A double-take of our bliss
Rolling 'round . . . your eyes
While my fingers tingle
        Your prize

Your red hair shimmers ~~
In the burn of firelight's song
I stroke your crimson curls
You're the master of where I belong

The traction of
Your slinky blue dress
As I slip within . . .
My lustful caress
        Your ivory smooth skin
        Invites me in
        My Dreamgirl

The scent of liquor
On our breath
Mingles with
The flickering sweat
Tongues to our passion
So sensual and wet
Incite a fever's glow

We just flow
In the slow . . .
Night of knowing

It is so . . . so—evidenced
By the plight of your sigh
        I am hung
            On the silence
As our moans die

And I melt
        Like hot jello
In the fold
        Of your mellow

On this night
        Of delight
With you
        In blue

My blue dress Lover—

Love is like
    a pot of gold
        you've finally found

But it's actually
    foil wrapped
        chocolate coins

It makes your mouth water
　　tastes so sweet
　　　　but melts away

Love is like
　　an ice cube
　　　　in the sun

You hold it
　　in your hand
　　　　and it feels solid

But it's cold . . .
　　and melts
　　　　right through your fingers

The mirror—cracked
leaves images distorted
of love's broken dreams
of sliding-down schemes

and visions of grandeur
that made me meander
to wonder in awe
what it is that I saw

before this old mirror
　　was cracked

The sunset—gone
leaves an image so warm
of dewdrops that melt
of feelings I felt

and visions of love
you shared here with me
which shone with the sun
when our day had begun

before this lush sunset
　　　　was gone

The music—heard
shines harmony still
of experiences shown
of memories known

and visions of song
inspiration brought along
my heart didn't know
. . . I wanted to show

before this clear music
　　　　was heard

The dream—reborn
shines brightly at me . . .
of kneeling at the ocean
of love in motion

and visions of you
I cherish in time
a heart song so real
I never could feel

before this love dream
        was reborn.

It's hard
Don't you know
I loved you so
But I just can't stay here
Anymore.

We've gone through this pain
So many times
But this time the wounds
Are just too sore.

I'm so tired
That I'm weary
It's just no good
Can't we say I love you
And let go like we should?

We've grown a lot together
That's what love is for . . . they say
But like we said in the beginning
If we grow apart
Then it must be okay.

Because growth is what matters
Things always change
I wanted to grow . . . with you
But it's not mine to arrange.

So come share another sunset
        With me
Just one more sunset
Before we go
After all . . .
It's the way we started
Now it could be
        Our afterglow.

If we've outgrown our welcome
Let's just leave it and say
We part as we started
True friends
Growing our own way.

I need to get on
With my own life now
And look beyond troubled times
We've both got a lot
To share . . . somewhere
But in a love
That truly rhymes.

So share another sunset
        With me
Just one more sunset
Before we go

After all . . .
It's the way we started
Now it could be
        Our afterglow.

In my heart
I've already left
You pushed me away
. . . Long ago
I kept on hoping
Something would change
. . . But it just rearranges.

So come share another sunset
        With me
Just one more sunset
Before we go
After all . . .
It's the way we started
Now it could be
        Our afterglow.

BLACK TIGHTS —

EROTIC THOUGHTS —

DREAMS OF PASSION —

FORGET ME NOTS —

PEACHES & CREAM

Waves of passion
wash over me
wondrous . . .
they seem to be

Sweat and desire
smells like peaches on fire
skin soft as cream
it's a dream

Life is a forest
I run through the trees
you are the stream
      I come to

Trickle drops on me
one at a time
cool me . . . quench me
make me feel fine

To drink
to swim
to quench this longing thirst
      of desire

—You set me on fire

Glad to be alive
just to feel you
ride beside me
      inside me

Waves of passion
wash over me
wondrous . . .
they seem to be

Sweat and desire
smells like peaches on fire
skin soft as cream
it's a dream

To see you sparkle
So bright
Rainbow moondrops
—Shoot
From inside your eyes
Mysterious princess

Moonbeams cry
On the ocean breeze
Take me . . .
To the sigh of relief
This day is done . . .
Turn the page on this one

Fire on high
Gone to rest
Heaven sent
A holy guest
To save you
On your lonely quest

As I spill . . . into my pillow
Headed for the pot-o-gold
        In my dreams
Where the priceless
Purple princess
Participates in passion

In the vision
        Of my memory
                I still see you
In your tight
        Leopard-skin
                Mini-dress

I still remember
        That first sake
                You bought me
To melt the ice
        Of our first meeting
                And caress

To hold that vision
Near me
To feel your warmth
Speak out to me
To touch . . .
And feel your essence
Wash all over me
Again . . . Sumika

Sumika . . .
The flower
Bond of ancient power
Sumika
You are the vision
Essence of the rose

Sumika . . .
On fire
Oriental desire
Important song
Of truth . . .
What you compose

Pure fragrance . . . that lingers
Long after you are gone
Smooth as silk
Gentle to touch
Your lily-white skin

Kisses . . .
Sparkling fireflies
Of bottomless desire
Each one a tingle
To my senses
Deep within

If only you knew
How I long for you
In my dreams
I touch your spirit
Deep inside

If only you knew
How I hunger
When I even think of you
I want you so damn bad
I have no pride

Sumika . . .
The flower
Bond of ancient power
Sumika
You are the vision
Essence of the rose

Sumika . . .
On fire
Oriental desire
Important song
Of truth . . .
You always sing

Oriental
        Mystic
                Maiden
Flower princess . . .
Climb the misty mountain
Of my heart

Over the top . . .
To the sunshine
That is endless
I could show you joy
Right from the start

Butterflies that land
On cherry blossoms
Surely they would tell
If they could fly

Anywhere . . . but only inside me
Oh how they would guide me
Back into that place
Inside your sigh

Sumika . . .
The flower
Bond of ancient power
Sumika
You are the vision
Essence of the rose

Sumika . . .
On fire
Oriental desire
Important song
Of truth . . .
That you compose

BLACK TIGHTS —

EROTIC THOUGHTS —

DREAMS OF PASSION —

FORGET ME NOTS —

PRISCILLA'S *ESCAPE*

Far from the worries
Of urban city madness
Away from heartbreak
      Loneliness
         Sadness

There's a place to slip into
. . . Like a crack in time
There's a woman waiting there
With a hunger in her eyes

Priscilla's *Escape*
Is the scent of a dream
A silky black-haired
Rhythm machine
Come for a little while
Stay for a lifetime
Escape with me
      On the dreamline

Hypnotize me
With those dark piercing eyes
Roll me again
With your firm brown thighs

Olive complexion erotica
Don't know where she got it
      But she's got it!

The sweat of *Escape*
Covers your body

Hold me closer
Take me home

Feel the passion
My flushed-heated kind
Embarrassed . . . not me
I'm blinded

Just caught in your spell
        You see
And the rhythm you weave . . . so well
        With your body
Materialize
        My dream
Be the peaches
        In my cream

Priscilla's *Escape*
Is the scent of a dream
A silky black-haired
Rhythm machine
Come for a little while
Stay for a lifetime
Escape with me
        On the dreamline

Hypnotize me
With those dark piercing eyes
Roll me again
With your firm brown thighs

Olive complexion erotica
Don't know where she got it
        But she's got it

As the curtains of night
. . . Unfold
We sneak between the tents
. . . Untold

To those whose watchful eyes
. . . Might see
Something they say
. . . Just shouldn't be

Creep ever so softly
. . . My dear
For this is one thing
. . . Their ears should not hear

The sound of our heartbeats
. . . So near
As our souls come together
. . . Right here

Plain Jane . . .
With her poodle
Walking down the breeze-way
Underneath it all
You can see
She's got a lovely sway

Covered with a skirt
Past her knees
Long stockings on her feet
She doesn't seem the kind ... really
You think you'd want to meet

But there's something about her sway
That makes me gaze her way

She's beautiful ...
Underneath it all
Hey Plain Jane
Do you wanna ball

Baby ...
I've been through it
I can take it
Or leave it
But if you want to
... Do it
I'll believe it

Plain Jane ...
Wants to come out and play
What do you say
Let's make it

Plain Jane ...
You make my day
Any way you shake it

Plain Jane ...
With her poodle
Glances demurely my way

Hair out of the '50s
And a sweater
On a day like today

Something in her eyes
Makes me want to get closer
Eluding to playfulness
Her wanton sashay

She's beautiful . . .
Underneath it all
Hey Plain Jane
Do you wanna ball

Baby . . .
I've been through it
I can take it
Or leave it
But if you want to
. . . Do it
I'll believe it

Plain Jane . . .
Wants to come out and play
What do you say
Let's make it

Plain Jane . . .
You make my day
Any way you shake it

You look so good in your Mercedes
the sun shows through
            your dress
as I pass . . . I tell you so
you look at me and smile
. . . shyly

I look ahead . . .
and almost rear-end a cop!
as you pass me by
            laughing
the sun shining through
to your tan lines
on this sunny Sunday

I find a lucky quarter
. . . in the grass
daisies flipping all around
you focus your camera
to the ground
then focus your lens on me
as you sit there
in your tight blue jeans
on the park bench

Sunny Sunday women
are everywhere
it must be spring fever
            late

You puff on your cigarette
then pause to draw pictures
of passing-by people

you get up
walk away
with a summery smile

I get to my car
see you on the stone stairs
        writing
as I drive by whistling a tune
You look up with bright eyes
straight into mine
then down again to your words
as I drive away
on this sunny Sunday

Sunny Sunday women
are everywhere
summer adds a certain spring
        to their gait

. . . But I'm late

37

BLACK TIGHTS —

EROTIC THOUGHTS —

DREAMS OF PASSION —

FORGET ME NOTS —

LACEY

Love to hear from you
Can't wait to see you write
Whether it's about true love
Or travails of your latest plight

You really can't get it wrong
It's all about your muse
Sometimes your moving words are winners
. . . Sometimes you lose

It's all in fun
You know
Poetry people
Have a special glow

Lacey . . . pink and white
Intricate patterns unite
In your awesome aura
Butterflies take flight

Long blond curls
On a poetry girl
Graceful beauty
Soft as lace

When I see you
Come at me
. . . I melt
All over the place

Smooth music is your rhythm
The choices you make . . . divine
You dance into the mood of it
Walking a racy line

Hover over me once more
As I stare into your eyes
. . . Of wonder
The nape of your neck
Is so damn warm
I think of you down under

Part of the poetry process
Is every experience you learn
Each new *write* makes you stronger
You grow with every page you turn

Get that golden pen out
Take a look around
Your muse is bound to smile on you
So don't ever set your pen down

It's all in fun
You know
Poetry people
Have a special glow

Lacey . . . pink and white
Intricate patterns unite
In your awesome aura
Butterflies alight

Long blond curls
On a poetry girl

Graceful beauty
Soft as lace

When I see you
Come at me
. . . I melt
All over the place

Hover over me once more
As I stare into your eyes
. . . Of wonder
The nape of your neck
Is so damn warm
I think of you down under

The longed-for love song
Of winter's brazen chill
Is there when I gaze
At firelight in your eyes

In your grazing kisses
        I see
Magical moments
Caught between thoughts
And embraces

In the traces of your lilting . . . fingers
Warm on my scruffy face
I melt into summer getaways

No longer nipped
By winter's brittle freeze

I see the reflection
Of love's passioned moments
The smolder in my gaze
Of what is sure to come . . .

Blanket bliss
And embered lips
Pressing all our winter worries
        Away

As you quiver . . . moisten
To my touch

Ever since we've met
I've had this strong urge
to eat strawberries
  fresh
    nourishing
      effervescent

Each kiss
like a snowflake's
unique pattern floating
  softly
    in the air
      then landing

Each a small
but integral part
of a soft
  white
    fluffy
      feather-bed

Each but a small
patch
in the quilt
  becoming
    our life
      together

One full of days
fresh for picking
strawberries
  you are
    still blossoming
      on the vine

Derogatory remarks
shattered dreams
broken hearts
perhaps were all to mold me
make me worthy for this moment
to receive and accept
        more freely
this love that comes so easy
that I thought would never come

The last laughers
hip shooters
crap table smackers
I thank them all
because they helped me
        surrender
so I can be here right now
        just here
                to love you

Okay . . .
you've got me doin' it
I'm inspired once again
I smell your fragrance in the air
everywhere I go
I momentarily measure
        our embrace
you catch my breath
and I catch yours

The subtlety of our oneness
springs up so naturally
like a geyser
gushes forth
it pours and pours
I'm like . . .
once-moist cracked ground
—sop it up
can't get enough

That's why I'm asleep
then awake
tired . . .
then inspired
I may be razzled
I'm certainly bedazzled
but not frazzled
　　　by loneliness
　　　　　anymore

A single long-stemmed rose,
brought by you as an offering:
　　a token,
a symbol of reconciliation,
still stands dried,
perfectly preserved
　　in memory,
awaiting your return
from the misunderstood
　　silence
of your self-imposed isolation
from the love that was just learning
to share, express, caress
—compassion, faith—
beginning to trust
　　enough
that it could be
　　trusted
to be there when needed
and it almost succeeded,

but time leaves love dry,
brittle, still, dusty,
   a memory
like the rose
and the nights without you;
still, silent, starless,
breaking the dawn
out there somewhere—
where you share this beautiful
   morning,
          this lonely mourning.

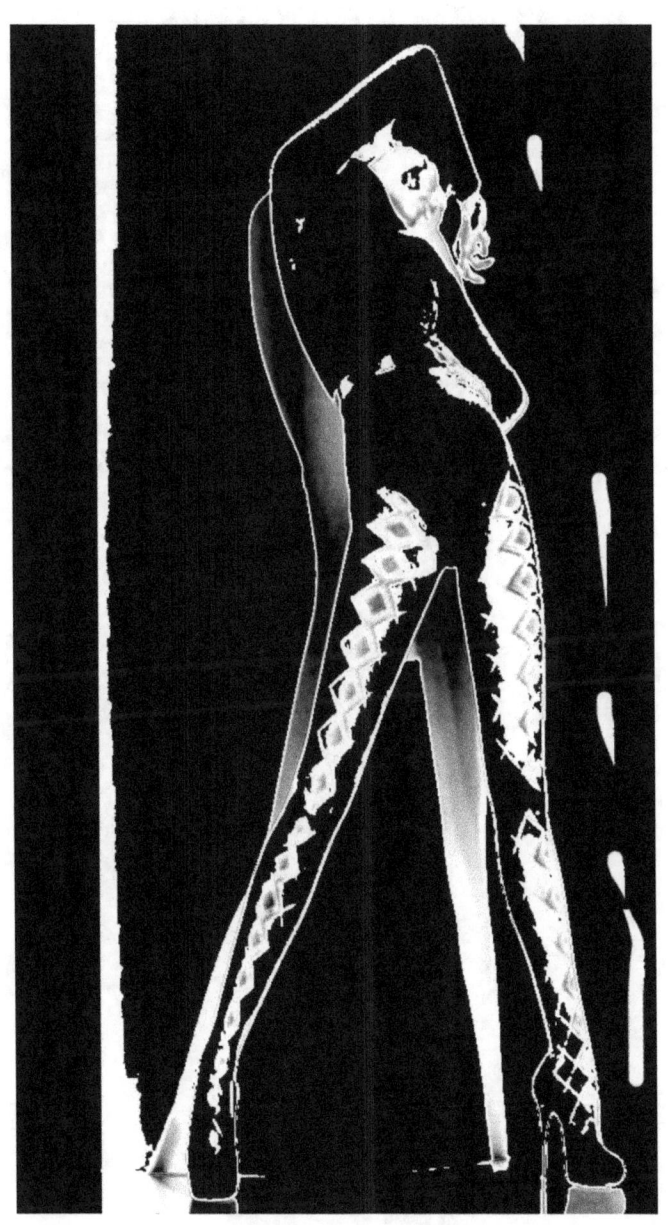

BLACK TIGHTS —

EROTIC THOUGHTS —

DREAMS OF PASSION —

FORGET ME NOTS —

BURNING LED

HARD AS NAILS

       POUNDING

THE SCREAMING ANGEL

       PUMMELS THE CROWD

THE PROFOUND REKNOWN

       SOARING OVER IT ALL

. . . AS YOU

RELINQUISH IN MASS

       THE KASHMIR YOU INHABIT

YOUNG GIRLS

       MELT IN YOUR MOUTH

LED TO THE BURNING . . .

       HONEY DRIPPING

       ALL THE WAY HOME

SHAHNAH—

Shahnah—
  Like the wind
    That rules the sky

Soft and tender
  Or roaring
    As you fly

Shahnah—
  Old soul
    Leading spirits high

Nothing can top the sparkle in your eye

For a woman
  You're so young
    You taste so sweet

Softly spoken
  Supple lips
    Your kisses can't be beat

Mature you are
  Diamond star
    Clear spirit of the sun

So young
    And yet . . . so old
        A new life you've just begun

Shahnah—
    Like the wind
        That rules the sky

Soft and tender
    Or roaring
        As you fly

Shahnah—
    Old soul
        Leading spirits high

Nothing can top the sparkle in your eye

Love me
    Take me
        Love me

Feel me . . . Love

Take me
    Love me
        Hold me

Feel me . . . Love

Shahnah—
    Like the wind
        That rules the sky

Nothing can top that sparkle . . . in your eye

Beautiful music
Was made just for you
You sleep like an innocent child
I call you my girl
There's something inside you
Seems a bit wild

The wave of your hair . . .
Like the curl on the waves of the sea
I love the way you gaze at me

You're sweet and supple
Like a seventeen-year-old bronze beauty
You see . . .
You're even in my dreams

The inquisitive blink of your lashes
Reminds me of a cheshire cat
I love to ponder . . .
The curves of your body
You giggle with dimples
I like you like that

Eyes so clear
They sparkle like starlight
You're warm when we mingle
You hold me so tight

You're sweet and supple
Like a seventeen-year-old bronze beauty
You see . . .
You're even in my dreams

I yearn for your call
That swelter you've got
I drip when you love me
With your feelings so hot

We're honest when we speak
My heart feels strong
We hold hands when we sleep
We meld for so long

We belong together
I love the way you moan
You even do that in my dreams
How quickly we have grown

I watch you sleep
Curled up in a ball
How natural it seems
I love it all

You're sweet and supple
Like a seventeen-year-old bronze beauty
You see . . .
You're even in my dreams

Tiny as the seeds of rain,
lush and green the vast terrain.
A deep ocean sky foggy smeared,
high above the clouds have cleared.

Pigtails prance so near me now,
green carpet coats the lover.
Different colored smiles allow
much to be uncovered.

So near and yet untouchable,
to read you like a book . . .
which needs its pages slowly turned
to the window where you look.

Vast the shroud, like spilled whipped cream,
conjures up your colored dream
into something showable.
Is your magic knowable?

Mount in dream time proud and private,
brave your knowledge and describe it.
Read the rather boring score . . .
I would have you give up more.

Leather lounging shook me up,
drench me in your buttercup.
Captured colors braided close,
leave me with an overdose.

Double cover, softened layers
signify the lustful players.
Mounds of luscious hand-clasped moans
draw me to your stranger zones.

As we languish between shaking sleep
and rumbling awake,
the sky curls like layers on a lake,
or clothes . . . on a newly bloomed rose.

      Your sigh is the reason
      . . . I suppose.

Open the cabinet,
discover your stash.
Sprinkle in rose water
with a hot flash.

Fun on a dime
just in time to discover . . .
it's easy you know
because . . . you're my lover.

Snow-capped silhouettes
linger below,
melt in a moment
from the view of your glow.

How can we linger now
when we drop down? . . .
for dream time is over
and we've . . . touched . . . the . . . ground.

You say you love me
. . . oh so much.
You want to experience
. . . my every touch
that I might have to give,
that you might have to feel.

Yet you want to discover
what more might be out there;
to uncover and feel
all the world has to offer.
Your young lust longs,
your body aches to describe . . .
what another young lover
might have deep inside.

How can I decide
to keep or let you go?
How can I live with
what I might have to know?
How can I taste
your caresses so sweet
that will leave me stale
with a love incomplete?

Sweet and tempting,
your words stick in my throat,
"I want you, I need to . . .
feel all that you have,
but I want to feel
the whole world!
It's mine to explore!"
The catch strikes so deep,
don't you know?

How can I keep you
but let you go?
My world isn't ready
for a relationship like this.
Or is it just . . .
I cannot stand
what it is I will no longer
experience first hand,

as I burn for your kisses
and long for your touch . . .
afraid I might lose you,
who I treasure so much.

How can I decide
to keep or let you go?
How can I live with
what I might have to know?
How can I taste
your caresses so sweet
that will leave me stale
with a love incomplete?

It's hard sometimes
Letting you go
I was looking for a full-time love
You know
And you were looking
To find yourself

But it's always fun
Watching you grow
Observing self-discovery
Makes my insides glow
Does it show

So go on flower
Bloom . . .
I'll just dance
Around my room
And tingle inside
For the knowing
Go on flower
Bloom . . .

It's awkward sometimes
When you call
And I have nothing
To say at all
'Cause I know
You're just looking
To find yourself

There's so much
I'd really like
        To say
But it all stems
From yesterday
So I let it go
And watch you . . .
Looking to find yourself

So go on flower
Bloom . . .

I'll just dance
Around my room
And tingle inside
For the knowing
Go on flower
Bloom . . .

I went walkin'
Lookin' for freedom one night
And I ran into you
In your long black dress
You were lookin' just right
And I knew what I wanted to do

But before I could speak
You saw the ring on my hand
You put your finger to my lips
You took command
And you said . . .

"You better get on home
Before it's too late
Before the sun stops shinin' on you
Better get on back
To freedom's gate
Where true love's waitin' to see you"

But I was thinkin' . . .
That you and I might get along

I'm just a man
And you look so fine . . .
We couldn't do much wrong

"You think you want your freedom
But you don't know where it's found
Don't know you've already got it
Don't know where you are bound"
You said . . .

"You better get on home
Before it's too late
Before the sun stops shinin' on you
Better get on back
To freedom's gate
Where true love's waitin' for you"

Hey . . .
Superstition man
Layin' your line on my woman
But don't try to lay it
On me, man

'Cause I've seen that plan
Before . . .

Hidin' around
Behind my door
Waitin' for me to go out
Then creepin' around

Behind my back
Fillin' my woman with doubt

Hey . . .
Superstition man
Takin' it while you can
But the only way you can get it
Is by sneakin' in
On another man's woman

Listen to me . . . woman
Don't you fall under his spell
'Cause superstition's gonna getcha
You know damn well

So . . .
Rock it in the socket
Before you walk out my door
. . . Honey
Rock it in the socket
Like you never did before

Rocket in the socket
Wake up baby . . . take me
Rocket in the socket
Earthquake woman . . . shake me

. . . Once more

Where are you
My Tam Valley Queen
Where are you
My hunger
Do you ever wonder
Why I linger

Just waiting . . .
For the mingling of love

Superstition man
Is gonna take you
Shake you up
And fake you
. . . Break it in the end

You always seem
To forsake it

If you throw our dream away
. . . Baby
It may not come back tomorrow
And it may leave you lonely
With only aching sorrow

So go already
. . . If you're goin'
        Go
And don't look back

I'll just sit here
Watchin' the sky die . . .
Blue turnin' black

Rock it in the socket
Before you walk out my door
. . . Honey
Rock it in the socket
Like you never did before

Rocket in the socket
Wake up baby . . . take me

Rocket in the socket
Earthquake woman . . . shake me

. . . Once more

Two blue stars . . .
Two white candles
—Burning
It's time to face the judgement
Of your yearning

Mystical magic . . .
It's in the eye
Of the beholder
Are you growin' wiser
Or just gettin' older

Don't smoulder my fire
        Just yet
For I have much to say
You can't seem to grasp the meaning
Inside your disarray

You say . . .
you need some space
your own time to go and play
and . . .
you never know how much you love me
til you go away

So go already
. . . If you're goin'
        Go
And don't look back

I'll just sit here
Watchin' the sky die . . .
Blue turnin' black

But . . .
Rock it in the socket
Before you walk out my door
. . . Honey
Rock it in the socket
Like you never did before

Rocket in the socket
Wake up baby . . . take me
Rocket in the socket
Earthquake woman . . . shake me

. . . Once more

One lonely sailboat
hammers at the wind
sunlight dims
on the Venus horizon

Clouds on the wall
not real at all
except . . .
in my imagination

I do not have to know
anything . . . you say
but I feel a need to know

64

Is it unreasonable
that I should want
. . . to know
where you are

And isn't it
. . . so usual
that I have no way
of reaching you

What if I wanted to call
what if I were to fall
well . . . it's too late
I fell for you long ago

How do you reach
the unreachable
how do you teach
the unteachable

I'm so lonely
I could die
oh . . .
unreachable you

One lonely sailboat
hammers at the wind
sunlight dims
on the Venus horizon

BLACK TIGHTS —

EROTIC THOUGHTS —

DREAMS OF PASSION —

FORGET ME NOTS —

LOVE DOLL

You're a love doll . . .

Self-inflated

With your botox lips

And plastic tits

Don't you just beat all

You're just a love doll

Paint your face

With the latest craze

Can't see too clearly

In your oxycodone haze

You're a love doll

Can't touch your soul

'Cause the makeup's on too thick

You never lose control

But you're not too quick

. . . You're a love doll

You can't see the world
You're so lost in your cloud
You'd rather upload
Than experience life

You can't look around you
You're stuck . . .
Your little hot box
Your fingers just pluck

You never look up . . .
To look around
There's a whole world out there
That could astound you

You're missing your own life
It's passing you by
All you can see
Is the cloud in your eye

I can almost hear
What you're thinking . . .
"Don't look at me!
Talk to the cloud!"

iCloud—MyCloud—YourCloud

You know big brother
Is watching you

When your future is . . .
Talk to the box

It's so . . . two seconds ago
. . . And it's trending

Upload the future . . . now
Before it gets away
Store it in the cloud
Your only memory

All you want to do
Is whip it into a frenzy
Diss it with a swirl
Dance it til it drops

The thrill of the moment
Is all you live for . . .
it's all you got

So just . . .

     Upload

The real world
Doesn't hold
Enough memory

No experiences
To store away
For download
On a rainy day

All you hear
All you see
All you want . . .
Is your hot little box

I can almost hear
What you're thinking . . .
"Don't look at me!
Talk to the cloud!"

iCloud—MyCloud—YourCloud

—OurCloud

There are no natural
Women left
They all want to look
Like stars

With black eyebrows
Blonde hair and red lips
They look more like the flies
In the bars

But maybe
That's just what they want
With their *ho* lingo
And tattoo bling

They stare like they wanna
Kick yer ass . . .
And think you are gay
When you sing . . . unless you scream!

But they don't hold a candle
To the women in the '60s
With their hair flowing down
Wearing spring Levi blues

With little or no makeup
And natural breasts too
Smelled of peaches . . .
And nature renewed

If the CEO's limo
Comes knockin'
At your door . . .
You'll be at his beck and call

Though you claim to be
Women of power
You're not in touch
With your feelings at all

It's sad what the media
Crams on you
—It's plastic
And faddy . . . and unreal

It only has to do
With image and money
Not about what
You really feel

Stylish and stone-faced
With cleavage to spare
Polished and perfect
You strut it with flair

Fashion and fiction
Your knowledge of those
Does far more to please you
Than what I compose

It's your pantyhose purpose
With thongs that glitter
Toenails that shine
Hands on your twitter

That make up the world
You spend all your time in
You're a consummate consumer
With a corporate grin

And if I sound jaded
It's just that I care
For the natural woman
Who is hiding in there

Who is longing deep down
To be free of this clamor
That traps you and bleeds you
This masquerade of glamour

That keeps you from being
Who you really are
If you could come back to earth
From your nebulous star

To be what you really
        Can be
To know what you really
        Believe

To love what it is
That you really want
Deep down it's for you
That I grieve

There's a natural woman
Who wants to let down her hair
Speak with real thunder
Show that she cares

Wipe off all that makeup
Take off all that bling
Uncover the song
That you sing . . .

        And with a big grin
        Declare you are free
        Of the plastic fantastic
        That you don't wanna be

                Anymore . . .

73

BLACK TIGHTS —

EROTIC THOUGHTS —

DREAMS OF PASSION —

FORGET ME NOTS —

THE DANCE OF ME & YOU

I am thinking of you right now
Are you thinking of me
I am thinking of the warmth
Where we could be

This feeling pours out of me
Your love feels so good
This inspiration . . . doesn't happen enough
I wish it would

You say you fall so easy
. . . You get hurt
But you've got to take the chance
You strike me sensless with your flirt

Don't you see now
Don't you see how
You've got to take the chance
Get up and dance

The dance of Me & You
Till the morning dew
The dance of Me & You
. . . Love anew

You are going your way
I am going mine
But we've got some time . . . you know
Time right now to grow

We're honest with each other
It's obvious to see
In any good relationship
It's got to be

Don't you see now
Don't you see how
You've got to take the chance
Get up and dance

The dance of Me & You
Till the morning dew
The dance of Me & You
. . . Love anew

Into your heart comes whirlwind romance
Taken in rapture that clings to the soul
Might you believe it was love at first glance
Look too close and you might lose control

Promise me anything . . . bring me some joy
Into this heart make the sight of you sing
Show me in some way I'm not just your toy
Sing me the passion that true love can bring

It's not just a little thing that I request
Melt me with moonbeams that shine from your eyes
Show me . . . you can move miles from the rest
Grant me the warmth of your gentle surprise

It shall fully give me the passion I seek
And I will then know love . . . the soul of your glow
As we tumble in ecstacy not for the meek
Your kiss on my lips will bring all love can know

In the fantasy reaches
Of our silver-glistened dreams
These moody metaphors
Reach out . . .
To touch our memories
And unite the streaming consciousness
Once more

Although the words we never said
May haunt us for all time
I'll not regret we ever met
I loved you in my prime

This song that comes so slowly
Reminds me of those years
The thrill of love
The sadness . . .
And even the lonely tears

Although I can't replace them
they'll live on in this song
We'll always be reminded
Of a timeless love so strong

In the fantasy reaches
Of our silver-glistened dreams
These moody metaphors
Still reach out . . .
To touch our memories
And unite the streaming consciousness
Once more
. . . With feeling

BLACK TIGHTS— *EPILOGUE*

We all have a story

    Where we came from

        Where we're going

            Those we loved

                And those . . .

                    Who came along

To become

    Part of our song

        It's how you get to be

            Strong

                And find out

                    Where you belong

I belong

    On this page

        Where I will always write

            About love

                And what I dream of

                  . . . And my Dreamgirls

GYPSY WRITERS

Gypsy writers on the wavelength
Spin their hearts upon the page
Freedom riders of the future
Ride the magic language waves

You can see them pour their hearts out
On the net around the world
Spreading images of truth . . .
Inspiration unfurled

Do you doubt the dreams you've made
As the muse designs you
Do you find your soul's been braved
As the verse reminds you

You roam the world with your wordsong
Imagination is where you belong
You land to lend a helpful pen
Then roam to do it again

Gypsy writers on the wavelength
Spin your hearts upon the page
Freedom writers of the future
Ride the magic language waves

*. . . and I would like to thank
all my Dreamgirls
for their inspiration . . .*

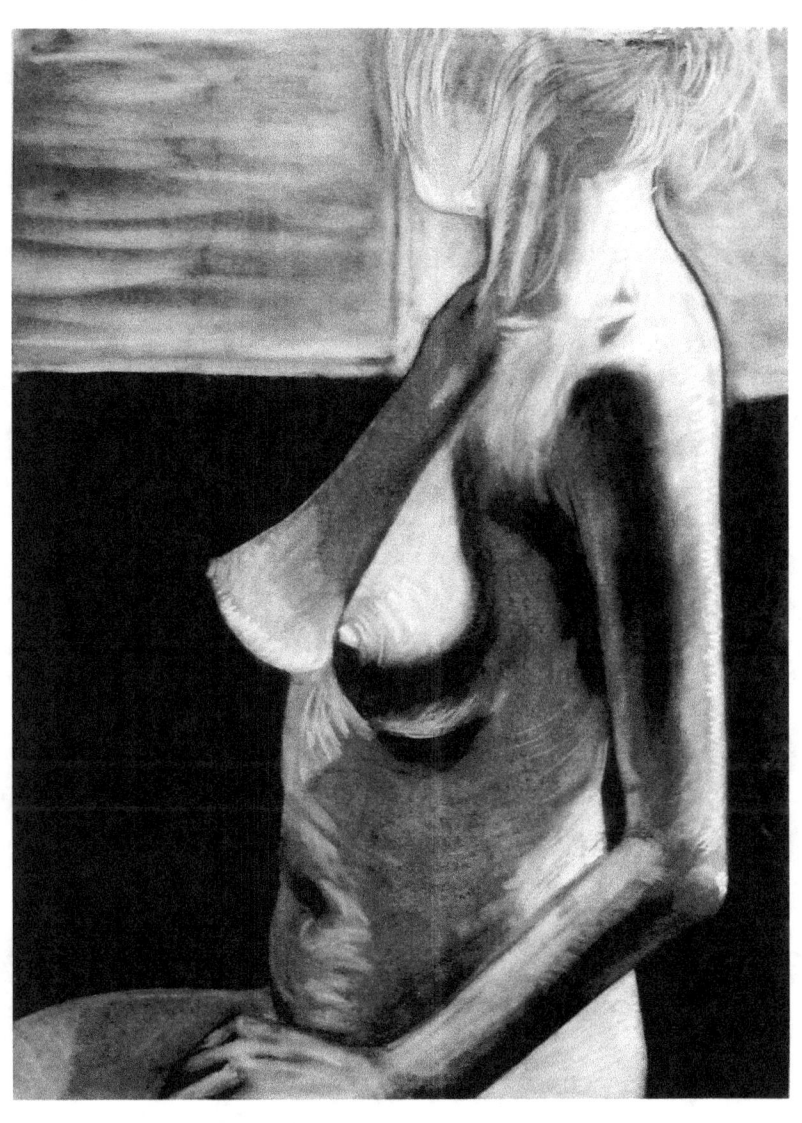

Bronze Affair
charcoal on paper
by C. Steven Blue, 1989

ABOUT C.S. BLUE

Poet, Musician, Artist — C.S. Blue stands outside the current conventions of poetry. He is a poet of the common language, a poet of the heart. Definitely a romantic, he's a lyrical/performance poet and his poetry often reads like a song. Steven reaches people with his heartfelt words; inspired poetry that people can relate to and understand.

Steven is retired from a 27 year career in Stage Production in Hollywood, California. He grew up on the streets of the 1960s. Much of his writing is influenced by those sensibilities, when peace, love and brotherhood were normal, everyday topics of discourse. He has hosted readings and open mics in both California and Oregon.

C.S. Blue now pursues his lifetime calling as a lyrical/performance poet in Eugene, Oregon, where he organizes and hosts many local poetry events, including the Eugene Public Library's Summer Reading Series Poetry Workshop and Poetry Showcase. He has four published books and a blog on his website, www.wordsongs.com.

www.ingramcontent.com/pod-product-compliance
Lightning Source LLC
Chambersburg PA
CBHW071339130626
46556CB00004B/1952